To Claire, Elliott, and Jack
—K.G.

To the Sullivans
—N.S.

Library of Congress Cataloging-in-Publication Data has been applied for.
ISBN: 0-8109-5974-7

Text copyright © 2006 Kes Gray
Illustrations copyright © 2006 Nick Sharratt

First published in Gread Britain by The Bodley Head Children's Books in 2000.

Printed and bound in Singapore
10 9 8 7 6 5 4 3 2 1

Harry N. Abrams, Inc.
115 West 18th Street
New York, NY 10011
www.abramsbooks.com

Abrams is a subsidiary of

LA MARTINIÈRE

Eat Your Peas

Kes Gray & Nick Sharratt

Harry N. Abrams, Inc., Publishers

It was dinnertime again and Daisy knew just what her mom was going to say, before she even said it. "Eat your peas," said Mom.

Daisy looked down at the little green
balls that were ganging up on her plate.
"I don't like peas," said Daisy.

Mom sighed one of her usual sighs. "If you eat your peas, you can have dessert," said Mom.

"If you eat your peas, you can have dessert and you can stay up for an extra half hour."

"I don't like peas," said Daisy.

"If you eat your peas, you can have dessert, stay up for an extra half hour, and skip your bath."

"If you eat your peas, you can have ten desserts,

 stay up really late, you don't have to take a

bath for two whole months,

and I'll buy you

a new bike."

"I don't like peas," said Daisy.

"If you eat your peas, you can have forty-eight desserts, stay up past midnight, you never have to take a bath again, and I'll buy you two new bikes and a baby elephant."

"I don't like peas," said Daisy.

"If you eat your peas, you can have 100 desserts,

you can go to bed when you want, take baths when you want, do what you want when you want, I'll buy you ten new bikes, two pet elephants, three zebras, a penguin, and a chocolate factory."

"I don't like peas," said Daisy.

"If you eat your peas, I'll buy you a supermarket stacked full of desserts,

you never have to go to bed again ever, or school

again, you never have to take

a bath, or brush

your hair, or clean

your shoes, or tidy your

bedroom, I'll buy you a bike shop, a zoo, ten chocolate

factories, I'll

take you to Superland

for a week and you can

have your very own

rocketship with double

retro laser

blammers."

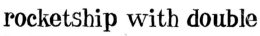

"If you eat your peas, I'll buy you every supermarket, candy store, toy store, and bike store in the world, seventeen swimming pools, you never have to go to bed again, or go to school, or take a bath, or brush your hair, or clean your shoes, or brush your teeth, or clean the hamster's cage, or clean your bedroom, or put the videos in yourself, or get dressed,

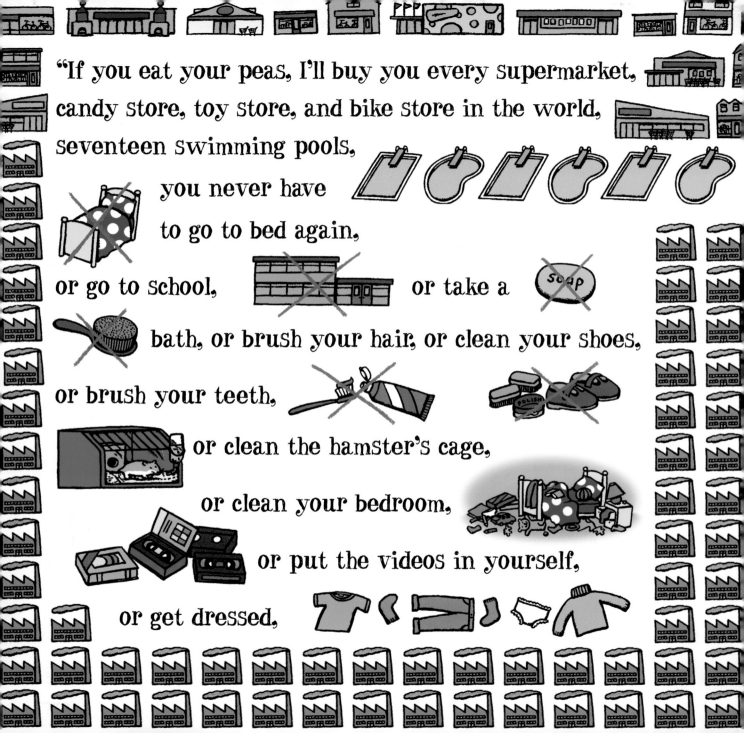

I'll buy you Africa and ninety-two chocolate factories, we'll move to Superland, you can have all the rocketships you want, I'll buy you the earth, the moon, the stars, the sun and . . . and . . . and . . .

"You really want me to eat my peas, don't you?" said Daisy.

"Yes," said Mom.

"I'll eat my peas if you eat your brussels sprouts," said Daisy.

Mom looked down at her own plate
and her bottom lip began to tremble.
"But I don't like brussels sprouts," said Mom.

"But we both like dessert!"